JUV
B
PAINE

To Caryn Wiseman and Rotem Moscovich for their rebel spirit
in support of these words—S.J.M.

For my family—E.F.

Special thanks to Dr. Jett Conner, Paul Myles, Heather Crowley,
Maria Elias, Big Sur Writing Workshop, SCBWI Western Washington,
and the team at Disney Hyperion. Huzzah!

Text copyright © 2018 by Sarah Jane Marsh
Illustrations copyright © 2018 by Edwin Fotheringham
All rights reserved. Published by Disney • Hyperion, an imprint of Disney Book Group.
No part of this book may be reproduced or transmitted in any form or by any means, electronic or
mechanical, including photocopying, recording, or by any information storage
and retrieval system, without written permission from the publisher. For information
address Disney • Hyperion, 125 West End Avenue, New York, New York 10023.
First Edition, May 2018
10 9 8 7 6 5 4 3 2 1
FAC-029191-18061
Printed in Malaysia

This book is set in 14-point ShipleyRegular, ShipleyRough,
1726 Real Espanola Regular, The Redlight/Fontspring
Designed by Maria Elias
The illustrations and hand-lettering were drawn by hand on a digital device.

Library of Congress Cataloging-in-Publication Data

Names: Marsh, Sarah Jane, author. • Fotheringham, Ed, illustrator.
Title: Thomas Paine and the dangerous word / by Sarah Jane Marsh ;
illustrated by Edwin Fotheringham.
Description: First edition. • Los Angeles : Disney/Hyperion, 2018.
Identifiers: LCCN 2016042503 • ISBN 9781484781449 (hardcover) • ISBN
1484781449 (hardcover)
Subjects: LCSH: Paine, Thomas, 1737-1809—Juvenile literature. • Paine,
Thomas, 1737-1809. Common sense—Juvenile literature. • United
States—Politics and government—1775-1783—Juvenile literature.
Classification: LCC JC178.V2 M37 2018 • DDC 320.51092 [B]—dc23
LC record available at https://lccn.loc.gov/2016042503

Reinforced binding
Visit www.DisneyBooks.com

Nobody expected much out of young Thomas Paine.

Born in England to a poor corset-maker and his wife, Thomas wasn't expected to go to school. But when he was seven, his parents scraped together enough money to send him.

School opened a new world to Thomas. He discovered the magic of words and how to shape his bouncing thoughts into poems, like the one he wrote at age eight upon the death of his pet crow:

Here lies the body of John Crow,
Who once was high but now is low;
Ye brother Crows take warning all,
For as you rise, so must you fall.

Words became a gateway to possibility. When his teacher told stories about the British navy, Thomas imagined his own battles on the salty sea. When he read books about a glorious new land called America, Thomas dreamed of sailing there.

But Thomas was not expected to sail to America. Or join the navy. Or even see an ocean at all. He was expected to be a corset-maker like his father and spend his life sewing women's underwear. So at age twelve, he was pulled out of school to begin work in his father's shop.

Just like that, Thomas's door to the world slammed shut.

Measuring. Cutting. Sewing. Thomas spent his teenage years hunched over his father's worktable threading whalebone into cloth. For seven . . . very . . . long . . . years.

But school had awakened Thomas to
life beyond corset-making. *"The mind once
enlightened cannot again become dark."*

One day, at age nineteen, Thomas saw an advertisement in the newspaper:

LONDON DAILY ADVERTISER

October 4, 1756

TO cruise against the French, the Terrible Privateer, Captain William Death. All Gentlemen Sailors, and able-bodied Landmen, who are inclinable to try their Fortune, as well as serve their King and Country, are desired to repair on board the said ship.

His government of Great Britain was at war with France. Suddenly, Thomas could envision a bold new future—a thrilling life at sea, just as he had dreamed.

Persuaded by words on a page, Thomas ran away to join Captain Death aboard the *Terrible*.

Worried that his son was making a deadly mistake, Thomas's father followed and urged him to stay ashore. Thomas agreed . . . for a while. Two months later, the *King of Prussia* set sail to cruise against the French.

This time Thomas was on board.

It was one thing
to imagine adventure,
but another to face it.

Six months later, Thomas strode down the
plank having achieved his dream of going to sea.
He decided to stay in London and pursue a safer
form of adventure—learning.

For two years he lived off his savings and
splurged on his mind, attending lectures on math
and physics, astronomy and philosophy. But big
thoughts did not pay the bills. Thomas needed to
find work.

For ten years Thomas struggled. He opened his own corset-making shop, but the business failed. He married a maid named Mary Lambert, but she died. He worked as a preacher and teacher, but earned little. He worked for the government as a tax collector, but was fired.

Still, the resilient Thomas could see the bright side. "I seldom passed five minutes of my life . . . in which I did not acquire some knowledge."

In humble obedience...

...add my thanks

...I humbly hope

no complaint

...given you no trouble

Thomas wrote the government to "*humbly beg*" for a second chance at his job. His polite words worked. They appointed Thomas as the tax collector in the lively town of Lewes, sixty miles south of London.

Thomas thrived in Lewes. He joined the town council and local committees. He met friends for bowling and ice-skating parties. And he married his landlord's daughter, Elizabeth Ollive.

Life was finally going his way.

His greatest joy, however, was the Headstrong Club. Every week, Thomas strode across town to join friends at the White Hart Inn. Dining on oysters and ale, they debated the issues of the day. Speaking with passion and conviction, wit and reason, Thomas quickly gained the reputation as "General of the Headstrong Club."

And every week, the winner of the evening's war of words would find a prize delivered on his doorstep—the Headstrong Book, his to keep until the next meeting.

Most often, it went to Thomas.

After years of trying, Thomas had discovered a talent: he had a way with words. When Thomas spoke, others listened.

Because...

Before long, Thomas was asked to use his talent to help others. His fellow tax collectors wanted Parliament—Britain's government—to improve their pay and working conditions. They asked Thomas to write the request.

Thomas threw himself into writing and distributing a twenty-one-page pamphlet to explain this injustice.

Parliament ignored his proposal. But the government did take one action. They fired Thomas. Again.

That spring, Thomas's life fell apart. All his failures were written in words, painfully clear.

He received notice of his firing:

Friday 8th April 1774
Thomas Paine, Officer of Lewes...
having been once before Discharged;
Order'd that he be again Discharged.

He ran out of money and sold his possessions to pay his bills:

SUSSEX WEEKLY ADVERTISER

April 11, 1774

To be Sold by AUCTION...
ALL the Household Furniture,
Stock in Trade and other
Effects of THOMAS PAINE.

And his marriage ended.

Bankrupt, unemployed, homeless, and alone. Thomas's dreams and hard work had come to nothing.

He would have to begin his world over. Again.

June 4, 1774
Whereas certain unhappy Quarrels and dissensions have arisen...
Thomas Paine and Elizabeth his Wife hath mutually agreed to live separate and apart.

Thomas returned to London. Just as he was looking for a new direction in life, a friend introduced him to someone who might be of help—the famous American, Benjamin Franklin.

Franklin was in London to help resolve the growing problems between Britain and her thirteen American colonies. Still, he made time to meet the bankrupt former tax collector from Lewes.

Thomas left his meeting with
a new plan and a special piece of
paper tucked in his pocket: a letter of
recommendation from Franklin.
Thomas was going to America.

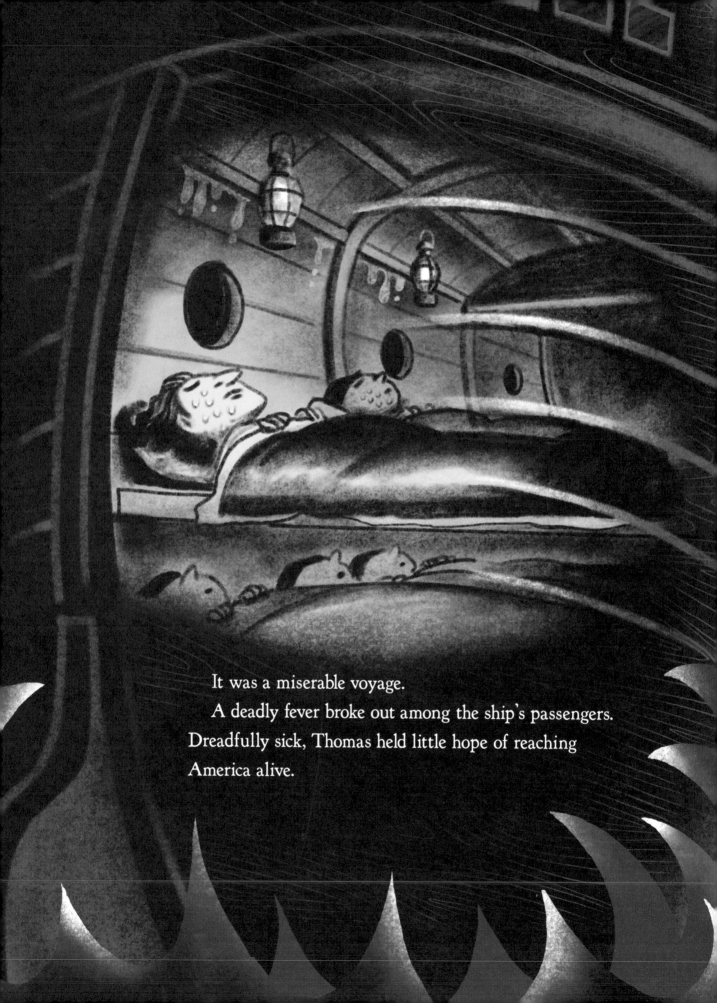

It was a miserable voyage.

A deadly fever broke out among the ship's passengers.
Dreadfully sick, Thomas held little hope of reaching
America alive.

After nine weeks, his ship arrived in Philadelphia. Thomas was barely conscious. When news spread that Thomas had a recommendation letter from Franklin, a local doctor hurried to carry him off the ship and arrange for his care.

Franklin's words likely saved Thomas's life.

When Thomas recovered, he set out to explore his new hometown of Philadelphia, ambling along the cobblestone streets. He noticed *"a happy something in the climate of America"*—a sense of freedom and possibility, what many people called liberty. The taverns and coffeehouses, however, bristled with debate about whether Parliament's new laws trampled on those liberties.

If there was one thing Thomas loved, it was a debate.

Harmony and union

No obedience is due
OUR RIGHTS...
...and liberties
Due respect
Unconstitutional
OUTRAGE
BOOKS

But outside the coffeehouse across from his home, Thomas could see people auctioned off like cattle. Slavery angered Thomas. Where was *their* liberty? Slavery was an injustice—an *"outrage against humanity"* and a direct contradiction to the freedom so cherished in America. *"Enslaving our inoffensive neighbors and treating them like wild beasts . . . how shameful are all attempts . . . to excuse it!"*

If there was one thing Thomas couldn't stand, it was injustice.

Soon, Thomas found an audience for his strong opinions. While browsing in a bookshop, Thomas struck up a conversation with the store's owner, who was launching a new magazine and needed an editor. Thomas was launching a new life and needed a job.

Their partnership was a success. With Thomas writing and editing, the *Pennsylvania Magazine* quickly became the most popular in the colonies.

THE
PENNSYLVANIA
MAGAZINE:
OR,
AMERICAN
MONTHLY MUSEUM
MDCCLXXV
VOLUME 1

husbands away from wives...

Not afraid to speak his mind, Thomas wrote
against slavery: ". . . _selling husbands away from
wives, children from parents . . . is this doing to
them as we would desire they should do to us?_"

His essay sent a ripple across Philadelphia. Five
weeks later, the Pennsylvania Abolition Society was
formed—the first antislavery organization in America.

Thomas was inspired. In America, his words made
a difference.

Just as Thomas was settling into his new life, "*the country . . . was set on fire about my ears.*"

A messenger galloped into Philadelphia with alarming news. Fighting had broken out between colonists and British soldiers in the Massachusetts towns of Lexington and Concord. Dozens of colonists were shot dead near their homes.

Thomas was shocked. As bad as he believed the British
government to be, he never imagined they would be *so rash and
wicked* as to attack their own people.

Everyone was on edge. The colonies were now at war with the mightiest empire in the world—their own government of Great Britain.

"It *was time to stir*," Thomas said. "It *was time for every man to stir*."

Outraged, Thomas picked up his own patriotic weapon—
his pen. He ranted against the injustice of Britain's government and
urged colonists to defend their liberties.

His words fell on deaf ears. Despite the growing violence, the colonists remained stubbornly loyal to their king. The newspapers and taverns were full of talk about reconciliation—how to resolve their *"unhappy differences"* and restore the harmony between Britain and her colonies.

But Thomas knew that privately some
people expressed a different desire. The desire
for American independence—cutting all ties
with Britain and creating a new nation of their
own. Thomas agreed with the quiet minority.
Independence was the only way America could
keep her liberties in the face of an angry,
punishing Britain.

If only the people weren't so afraid.

"Independence" was a dangerous word—so dangerous Thomas was not allowed to discuss it in the *Pennsylvania Magazine*. A friend suggested Thomas write a pamphlet on the subject. If anyone could write a persuasive argument for independence, he said, it was Thomas.

ndence

"The force with which it struck my mind and the dangerous condition the country appeared to me in . . . made it impossible for me, feeling as I did, to be silent."

It was time for the idea of independence to come out of the dark.

Dearly, dearly do we pay and ruin In America the law is King

Thomas began work on his pamphlet. Once again, he hunched over a table, but instead of sewing corsets he sowed seeds of revolution. Everything he wrote was in direct opposition to popular opinion. But as his pen scratched across the page, his passion grew.

Pamphlets were usually written in fancy words for the colonial elite; Thomas used "*language as plain as the alphabet.*" He wrote so common people could understand. Using wit, rage, and reason, the former General of the Headstrong Club attacked each of the deeply held beliefs that tied the colonists to Britain.

Over several months he wrote, edited, thought, and refined. He showed his drafts to friends, who worried for Thomas's safety. They advised Thomas to *"avoid by every means"* the dangerous word "independence."

Headstrong, Thomas ignored the advice. He used the word twenty-two times.

As Thomas finished his manuscript, he ended with a promise born from personal experience:

"We have it in our power to begin the world over again.... The birthday of a new world is at hand."

Thomas gave his seventy-nine-page manuscript to a Philadelphia printer, who courageously agreed to print a thousand copies.

The pamphlet was called *Common Sense*.
And on January 9, 1776, it went on sale.

COMMON SENSE:
ADDRESSED TO THE
INHABITANTS
OF
AMERICA
On the following interesting
S U B J E C T S.

COMMON SENSE:
ADDRESSED TO THE
INHABITANTS
OF
AMERICA
On the following interesting
S U B J E C T S.

News of the fiery pamphlet spread quickly. Members of Congress scurried to buy copies. And they couldn't believe their eyes.

In clear and brash terms, the author attacked the concept of kings, mocked the idea of reconciliation, and urged colonists to cast off their British government and boldly forge a new American nation governed by the people.

It was literary dynamite. Ideas whispered only in private conversation were now brazenly public, written in a style never seen before.

It was shocking.

It was explosive.

In just eleven days, *Common Sense* sold out. The printer rushed to print more.

John Adams and his cousin Samuel Adams sent *Common Sense* to their wives in Massachusetts. Thomas Jefferson received *Common Sense* as a present in Virginia. John Hancock, president of the Continental Congress, passed along *Common Sense* as *"a pamphlet which makes much Talk here."*

Like wildfire, *Common Sense* spread throughout the thirteen colonies, *"greedily bought up and read by all ranks of people"*— soldiers and shopkeepers, lawyers and farmers, all eager to read the sensational pamphlet on *"the frightful word* independence." Even those who couldn't read crowded into taverns and coffeehouses to hear Thomas's words read aloud.

"Common Sense *is working a powerful change*," wrote George Washington.

Thomas was amazed. The boy who once dreamed of sailing to America was now its most celebrated author. *"I have the pleasure of being respected and I feel a little of that satisfactory kind of pride that tells me I have some right to it,"* Thomas wrote his friend Franklin.

After *Common Sense*, the dangerous word didn't seem so dangerous anymore.

Inspired by Thomas's courage
and passionate reasoning, the people
began to speak out. . . .

They spoke out in newspapers:

NEWS

The Colonies must be independent or they are undone.

In letters:

I own myself convinced by the arguments on the necessity of separation.

And in town meetings:

Even those who disagreed spoke out in pamphlets of their own:

Could it be expected that all America would instantly take a leap in the dark ?... Is this Common Sense or common Non-Sense ?

Thomas had started the public
discussion of American independence.
In the spring of 1776, the debate raged up
and down the colonies. Brandishing his pen,
Thomas continued to write in support of
independence.

Six months after *Common Sense* appeared, bells rang throughout Philadelphia, summoning citizens to the yard of the State House to hear Congress's latest words read aloud:

... these United Colonies are,
and of Right ought to be
Free and Independent
States ...
all political connection
between Them and The
State of Great Britain,
is and ought to be
totally dissolved.

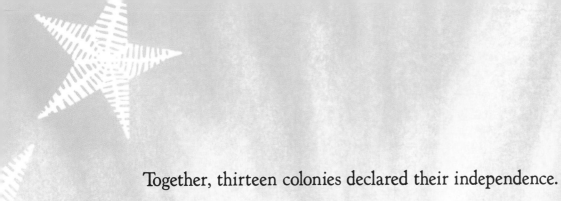

Together, thirteen colonies declared their independence.

Independence

Inspired by Thomas's unexpected words, America had
found her voice.

Thomas Paine and *The American Crisis*

Within six months of Congress's declaration, America was losing the war for independence. The ragged Continental Army was no match against the mighty British forces. By December 1776, even General Washington despaired, *"The game is pretty near up."*

In *"a passion of patriotism,"* Thomas wrote *The American Crisis* to urge frightened Americans not to give up hope.

"These are the times that try men's souls. . . ."
"Tyranny, like hell, is not easily conquered. . . ."
"The harder the conflict, the more glorious the triumph. . . ."

Thomas's words became a rallying cry. Legend says that General Washington ordered *The American Crisis* read aloud on Christmas night as the army prepared to cross the icy Delaware River for a final, desperate attack. Their surprising victory at Trenton boosted morale and became a turning point in the war.

Thomas wrote thirteen "Crisis" essays throughout the war, one in honor of each colony. When American spirits were low, Thomas was there to encourage them on.

On April 11, 1783, Congress officially declared the war over. Great Britain finally agreed to end the expensive conflict and recognize American independence. *"The times that tried men's souls are over,"* Thomas wrote in his last "Crisis" essay, *"and the greatest and completest revolution the world ever knew, gloriously and happily accomplished."*

Throughout the revolution, Thomas had been a tireless cheerleader for America. *"Without the pen of Paine,"* a Continental Army chaplain wrote, *"the sword of Washington would have been wielded in vain."* Or as John Adams later complained, *"History is to ascribe the American Revolution to Thomas Paine."*

What Happened to Thomas Paine?

Thomas Paine was America's first best-selling author. These days, we would say *Common Sense* went viral. The pamphlet went through twenty-five editions, was reprinted in newspapers, and by some estimates a hundred thousand copies passed among the American population of 2.5 million. In support of the revolution, Paine donated all his profits to the Continental Army.

Paine continued to publish his thoughts and opinions throughout his life. In 1787, fascinated by science, he left America and moved to England and France to work on his design for an iron bridge. Inspired by the growing French Revolution, Paine wrote *Rights of Man*, advocating natural rights and equality for everyone. His words fanned the flames of the rebellion and became an international best seller. (*"A share in two revolutions is living to some purpose!"* Paine wrote his friend George Washington.)

Although popular with the public, Paine's political views often put him in conflict with government leaders. He was outlawed in England and later imprisoned in France for ten months, where he narrowly escaped the guillotine.

Angry that President Washington did not arrange his rescue from prison, Paine wrote a scathing public letter to his former friend. That letter, and publication of *Age of Reason*, which challenged institutionalized religion, ruined Paine's reputation in America. He received a chilly reception when he finally returned to the United States at age sixty-five.

Despite his literary success, Paine struggled with poverty later in life. (To keep his writings affordable for everyone, he often charged only enough to cover the printer's paper and ink.) After a long illness, Paine died in 1809 at the age of seventy-two with little note of his death.

The power of Paine's pen was undeniable. His words inspired common people to become politically active in revolutions across two continents. John Adams wrote in 1805, *"I know not whether any man in the world has had more influence on its inhabitants or affairs for the last thirty years than Tom Paine."*

Legacy

"I never tire of reading Paine."
—Abraham Lincoln

The words of Thomas Paine live on as they continue to inspire new generations. Abraham Lincoln, Walt Whitman, and Thomas Edison were all fans of Paine. During World War II, President Franklin D. Roosevelt comforted the American people by quoting Paine. Decades before he became secretary of state, navy veteran John Kerry referenced Paine in his testimony to Congress against the Vietnam War. And in his 2009 inauguration speech, President Barack Obama concluded with these rousing words from Paine's *American Crisis:*

> *"Let it be told to the future world . . . that in the depth of winter, when nothing but hope and virtue could survive . . . that the city and the country, alarmed at one common danger, came forth to meet it."*

Over two hundred years later, Thomas Paine's powerful words still shine light and encourage us on.

Timeline

January 29, 1737

Thomas Pain is born to Joseph Pain and Frances Cocke in Thetford, England. (He later adds an "e" to his last name upon arrival in America.)

1749–1756

Thomas works as an apprentice to his father as a corset-maker.

1756

The Seven Years' War begins between Great Britain and France. The conflict spreads to America, where it is known as the French and Indian War.

1757

Thomas goes to sea aboard the privateer ship *King of Prussia*.

September 27, 1759

Thomas marries Mary Lambert. She dies a year later.

1759–1767

He works as a corset-maker, excise officer, preacher, and teacher.

February 19, 1768

Thomas is appointed to the job of excise officer in Lewes, England.

March 26, 1771

Thomas marries Elizabeth Ollive and helps run her family's store.

1772–1773

He writes and distributes *The Case of the Officers of the Excise*.

Spring 1774

Thomas is fired from his excise job, legally separated from wife Elizabeth, and becomes bankrupt.

September 5, 1774

The First Continental Congress meets in Philadelphia to organize a colonial response to Parliament's Intolerable Acts (or Coercive Acts).

November 30, 1774

Thomas moves to America from England. He arrives in Philadelphia aboard the *London Packet* with a letter of recommendation from Benjamin Franklin.

January 1775

Thomas is hired as editor of the *Pennsylvania Magazine*.

April 19, 1775

Fighting breaks out in Lexington and Concord between colonists and British troops.

May 5, 1775

The Second Continental Congress meets in Philadelphia.

June 17, 1775

British troops attack colonial forces at the Battle of Bunker Hill.

August 23, 1775

King George III declares the American colonies in rebellion.

January 9, 1776

Thomas publishes *Common Sense*.

January 9, 1776

King George's October 26 speech is printed in America, accusing the colonies of waging war *"for the purpose of establishing an independent empire."* He orders a large military force to America to maintain *"authority"* and *"submission."*

Spring 1776

Thomas writes *The Forester's Letters* in defense of *Common Sense.*

July 2, 1776

Congress votes for American independence.

July 4, 1776

Congress approves a written Declaration of Independence.

Fall 1776

Thomas serves as aide to General Nathanael Greene, writes war reports for newspapers, and is a frequent guest of General Washington.

December 19, 1776

He publishes *The American Crisis,* the first of thirteen essays to urge public support of the war.

December 25, 1776

General Washington crosses the Delaware River with his army for a victory in Trenton.

April 1777

Congress appoints Thomas secretary to the Committee for Foreign Affairs after a nomination by John Adams. Thomas later resigns the position after a political scandal.

Winter 1777

Thomas visits the Continental Army at Valley Forge.

November 2, 1779

Thomas is appointed clerk to the Pennsylvania Assembly.

1780

He travels to France with John Laurens, who is tasked by Congress to ask King Louis XVI for help financing the war.

September 3, 1783

The war ends with the Treaty of Paris. Thomas later spends three weeks relaxing as a houseguest of George Washington.

1784

In appreciation for his service to America, New York gives Thomas a farm in New Rochelle.

1785

Thomas begins work on a series of inventions, including a smokeless candle and an iron bridge.

1786

He publishes his opinions on an American banking crisis, including *Dissertations on Government; The Affairs of the Bank;* and *Paper Money.*

1787

Thomas moves to Europe, carrying another letter of introduction from Benjamin Franklin. He begins a twenty-year correspondence with Thomas Jefferson.

1791–1792

He writes *Rights of Man* in defense of the French Revolution.

1793

Thomas is arrested in France and jailed for ten months as a political prisoner. Future US president James Monroe arranges for his release.

1793–1795

He writes *The Age of Reason,* attacking organized religion.

1796

He writes *Agrarian Justice,* proposing a social welfare system.

1802

Thomas returns to America after fifteen years in Europe.

June 8, 1809

Thomas dies in New York City at age seventy-two and is buried at his farm in New Rochelle.

Selected Bibliography

Bell, J. L. "The Evidence for Paine as a Staymaker." Web log post. *Boston 1775*. 31 Oct. 2014. www.boston1775.blogspot.com.

Brent, Colin E., Deborah Gage, and Paul Myles. *Thomas Paine in Lewes 1768–1774: A Prelude to American Independence*. Lewes: PM Trading, 2009.

Conner, Jett. "The American Crisis Before Crossing the Delaware?" *Journal of the American Revolution*. Feb. 2015. www.allthingsliberty.com [see below].

Conway, Moncure Daniel, and William Cobbett. *The Life of Thomas Paine, with a History of His Literary, Political, and Religious Career in America, France, and England. To Which Is Added a Sketch of Paine by William Cobbett (hitherto Unpublished)*. New York, London: Putnam's, 1893.

Ferling, John E. *Independence: The Struggle to Set America Free*. New York: Bloomsbury, 2011.

Kaye, Harvey J. *Thomas Paine and the Promise of America*. New York: Hill and Wang, 2005.

Liell, Scott. *46 Pages: Thomas Paine*, Common Sense, *and the Turning Point to American Independence*. Philadelphia: Running, 2003.

Maier, Pauline. *American Scripture: Making the Declaration of Independence*. New York: Knopf, 1997.

Maier, Pauline. "Thomas Paine and American Independence." *Primary Sources: Workshops in American History*. www.learner.org.

Nelson, Craig. *Thomas Paine: Enlightenment, Revolution, and the Birth of Modern Nations*. New York: Viking, 2006.

Paine, Thomas. *The Complete Writings of Thomas Paine*. Edited by Philip S. Foner. New York: Citadel Press, 1945.

Ponder, Benjamin. *American Independence: From* Common Sense *to the Declaration*. Charleston, S.C.: Estate Four, 2010.

Rickman, Thomas Clio. *The Life of Thomas Paine, Author of* Common Sense, Rights of Man, Age of Reason, Letter to the Addressers, &c. &c. London: T. C. Rickman, 1819.

Williamson, Audrey. *Thomas Paine: His Life, Works and Times*. Edinburgh: T. & A. Constable, 1973.

Recommended Websites

Adams Family Papers. www.masshist.org/digitaladams/archive

Boston 1775. www.boston1775.blogspot.com

Founders Online. National Archives and Records Administration. www.founders.archives.gov

Journal of the American Revolution. www.allthingsliberty.com

Letters of Delegates to Congress 1774–1789. Library of Congress. http://memory.loc.gov/ammem/amlaw/lwdg.html

National Archives. www.archives.gov/historical-docs

Source Notes for Quotations:

"Here lies the body of John Crow..."
Thomas Clio Rickman, *The Life of Thomas Paine.*
(London: 1819, p. 34)

"The mind once enlightened cannot again
become dark." Thomas Paine, "A Letter
Addressed to the Abbé Raynal," *The Complete
Writings of Thomas Paine.* Edited by Philip S.
Foner. New York: Citadel Press, 1945. (Vol. 2, p. 244)

"To cruise against the French..."
London Daily Advertiser, October 4, 1756. (p. 2)

"I seldom passed five minutes..."
Rickman, *The Life of Thomas Paine*, p. 37.

"Humbly beg"
Paine, "Petition to the Board of Excise," London, July
3, 1766. *The Theological Works of Thomas Paine*
(J.P. Mendum: Boston, 1870). (Miscellaneous Letters
and Essays, p. 16)

"In humble obedience, no complaint..."
Paine, *"Petition to the Board of Excise."*

"Thomas Pain, Officer of Lewes..."
Moncure Daniel Conway and William Cobbett,
The Life of Thomas Paine, p. 29.

"To be sold by auction..."
Conway and Cobbett, *The Life of Thomas Paine*,
p. 30.

"Whereas certain unhappy Quarrels..."
Agreement for the separation of Thomas Paine
from his wife Elizabeth, Friends of the National
Libraries, East Sussex Record Office.
www.friendsofnationallibraries.org.uk

"There is a happy something in the climate
of America"
Paine, "The Magazine in America," *Pennsylvania
Magazine*, January 24, 1775. (Foner, Vol. 2, p. 1110)

"No obedience is due, our rights..."
Suffolk Resolves. *Journals of the Continental
Congress.* 17 Sept 1774.

"Outrage against humanity" and "Enslaving
our inoffensive neighbors..." and "...
selling husbands away from wives..."
Paine, "African Slavery in America," *Pennsylvania
Journal and the Weekly Advertiser.* March 8,
1775. (Foner, Vol. 2, p. 17–18)

"the country, into which I had just set
my foot, was set on fire about my ears"
and "so rash and wicked"
Paine, *The American Crisis VII.*
(Foner, Vol. 1, p. 143)

"It was time to stir"
Paine, *The American Crisis VII.*
(Foner, Vol. 1, p. 144)

"Unhappy differences"
*Journals of the Continental Congress,
1774–1789*, Worthington C. Ford et al, eds.
(Washington, D.C., 1904–37). 8 July 1775.

"The force with which it struck my mind..."
Paine, *The American Crisis XIII.*
(Foner, Vol. 1, p. 235)

"Abuse of power, ridiculous..."
Paine, *Common Sense.*

"language as plain as the alphabet."
Paine, "To the Public on Mr. Deane's Affair,"
January 8, 1779. (Foner, Vol. 2, p. 111)

"avoid by every means"
"To Thomas Jefferson from William Duane,
26 November 1802." Founders Online,
National Archives.

"We have it in our power to begin the world
over again. . . . The birthday of a new world
is at hand."
Paine, Common Sense. (Foner, Vol. 1, p. 45)

"Irresistible"
"General Charles Lee to George Washington, 24
January 1776." Founders Online, National Archives.

"Excellent"
"James Bowdoin to Mercy Warren." 23 March 1776.
Warren-Adams Letters, Vol 1. Massachusetts
Historical Society, 1917. p. 215.

"Unanswerable reasoning"
"From George Washington to Joseph Reed, 31
January 1776." Founders Online, National Archives.

"'Tis well done"
"William Robinson to Nathan Hale, 19
February 1776." Beinecke Library, Yale University.

"A great deal of good sense"
"John Adams to Abigail Adams, 19 March
1776." Founders Online, National Archives.

"Genius"
"John Adams to Abigail Adams, 28 April 1776."
Founders Online, National Archives.

"A pamphlet which makes much Talk here."
John Hancock to Thomas Cushing, 17 January 1776.
Smith, Paul H. et al, eds. Letters of Delegates to
Congress, 1774–1789. 25 volumes, Washington,
D.C.: Library of Congress, 1976–2000.

"greedily bought up and read by all
ranks of people" and "the frightful word
independence"
Josiah Bartlett to John Langdon, 13 January 1776.
Smith, Letters of Delegates to Congress,
1774–1789.

"Common Sense is working a powerful
change."
"From George Washington to Lieutenant
Colonel Joseph Reed, 1 April 1776." Founders
Online, National Archives.

"I have the pleasure of being respected and I
feel a little of that satisfactory kind of pride
that tells me I have some right to it"
Thomas Paine to Benjamin Franklin, October 24,
1778. (Foner, Vol. 2, p. 1154)

"The colonies must be independent or they are
undone."
"A Pennsylvania Countryman," Dunlap's
Pennsylvania Packet, May 13, 1776.

"I own myself convinced by the arguments of
the necessity of separation."
"To George Washington from Major General
Charles Lee, 24 January 1776." Founders Online,
National Archives.

"The inhabitants of Ashby . . ."
Peter Force, ed., American Archives, 4th Series
(Washington, D.C., 1833–46), VI: 706.

"Could it be expected that . . ."
"Cato to the People of Pennsylvania: On the improbability of receiving assistance from foreign powers, and against Independence." [1776-03-27] Cato. Peter Force, ed., *American Archives*, 4th Series (Washington, D.C., 1833-46), V: p. 514–15.

". . . these United Colonies are, and of Right ought to be Free and Independent States . . . all political connection between them and the State of Great Britain, is and ought to be totally dissolved."
Journals of the Continental Congress, 1774–1789, Worthington C. Ford et al., eds. July 2, 1776.

"the game is pretty near up."
"From George Washington to Samuel Washington, 18 December 1776." Founders Online, National Archives.

"a passion of patriotism"
"To the Honorable Henry Laurens, January 14, 1779." (Foner, Vol. 2, p. 1164)

"These are the times that try men's souls . . ."
"Tyranny, like hell, is not easily conquered . . ."
"The harder the conflict, the more glorious the triumph . . ."
Paine, *The American Crisis*. (Foner, Vol. 1, p. 50)

"The times that tried men's souls are over . . ."
Paine, *The American Crisis XIII*. (Foner, Vol. 1, p. 230)

"Without the pen of Paine . . ."
Harvey J. Kaye, *Thomas Paine and the Promise of America*. New York: Hill and Wang, 2005. p. 5.

"History is to ascribe . . ."
"To Thomas Jefferson from John Adams, 22 June 1819." Founders Online, National Archives.

"A share in two revolutions . . ."
"To George Washington from Thomas Paine, 16 October 1789." Founders Online, National Archives.

"I know not whether . . ."
"From John Adams to Benjamin Waterhouse, 29 October 1805." Founders Online, National Archives.

"I never tire of reading Paine."
Blumenthal, Sidney. *A Self-Made Man: The Political Life of Abraham Lincoln, Vol. I, 1809–1849*. Simon & Schuster, 2016. p. 66.

"Let it be told . . ."
President Barack Obama's 2009 Inaugural Address. (The president quoted Paine's *The American Crisis*, 23 December 1776. Foner, Vol. 1, p. 55)

"for the purpose of establishing an independent empire" and "authority" and "submission"
"The King's Speech on Opening the Session." Second Session of the Fourteenth Parliament, October 26, 1775.
The Parliamentary History of England from the Earliest Period to the Year 1803, Volume 18. London: Printed by T. C. Hansard, 1813. pgs. 696–97